Kay enjoyed a thirty-year career in education as a teacher, instructional coach, and principal. Now retired, she spends her time writing, gardening, exercising, attending sporting events, and spending as much time as possible with family and friends. She has a son and several nieces and nephews. She is an avid Dodger fan and proudly cheers on her alma mater, the University of Utah.

Melissa P.

Waterloaf in Shifting in and out of Control

Kay Oborn

AUSTIN MACAULEY PUBLISHERS™
LONDON • CAMBRIDGE • NEW YORK • SHARJAH

Ordering Information:
Quantity sales: special discounts are available on quantity purchases
by corporations, associations, and others. For details, contact the publisher
at the address below.

Publisher's Cataloging-in-Publication data
Oborn, Kay
Melissa P. Waterloaf in Shifting in and out of Control

ISBN 9781641829892 (Paperback)
ISBN 9781641829908 (Hardback)
ISBN 9781645366614 (ePub e-book)

Library of Congress Control Number: 2019916384

The main category of the book — JUVENILE FICTION / Action & Adventure / General

www.austinmacauley.com/us
First Published (2019)
Austin Macauley Publishers LLC
40 Wall Street, 28th Floor
New York, NY 10005
USA
mail-usa@austinmacauley.com
+1 (646) 5125767

This story is dedicated to my niece, Alexandra. The character of Melissa P. Waterloaf came to life when I made up stories to share with her when she was young.

I would like to acknowledge Miranda Howe for the first initial editing of the story. I would also like to acknowledge my mother, Millie, for listening to several drafts of the story and giving me lots of encouragement.

Melissa P. Waterloaf is an amazing young girl,
From her small brown freckles to her strawberry
blond curls.
She has sky blue eyes and red, rosy cheeks,
Her smile is cheery and memorable for weeks.

She often wears jeans, red sneakers,
and spotted socks,
She uses little bows to hold up her blond, reddish locks.
She is tall for her age and skinny as well,
She can outrun the boys and beat the school bell.

She works hard in school and keeps up her grades,
She turns in her homework even early some days.

Her family is average, as average as can be,
With two younger brothers, the siblings make a nice three!
Her mom teaches at a local elementary school,
Her dad is a lawyer who upholds the rules.
Her house is a rambler on South LaSalle Street,
She has her own room and keeps it quite neat.

Her dog is a small, white Shih Tzu, named Lou,
Who she takes everywhere, as good friends will do.

Her best friend is Suzy, she lives right next door,
They do everything together,
sometimes even their chores!
Suzy is an only child, she always wanted a sister,
So Melissa P. Waterloaf fits perfectly in her "that's
the perfect sister picture."

The girls are in the same class and share the
same age, They even share clothes,
whatever's the latest rage.
They play after school and on the weekends too,
They paint, sing, and dance, and play pretend school.

Once in a while they will disagree in some way,
Mostly about what they are going to play.
In fact, this was the case one day last summer,
Suzy wanted to play dolls, but Melissa
P. Waterloaf wanted
to do something funner.
[Funner isn't really a word,
but the girls say it all the time,
besides it fits in the story
and makes a perfect rhyme.]

"I've got it!" shouted Melissa P. Waterloaf,
as she pointed outside,
"Let's play in Grandpa's truck and pretend
we're on a ride."

Parked in the driveway was Grandpa's old, Chevy truck,
Melissa P. Waterloaf's dad often joked,
"You couldn't sell that thing for a buck."
But old or not, the girls loved that truck
as a place to play,
Their imaginations ran wild,
sometimes for half a day.

So out the door they ran and down the
stairs they raced,
With Lou following right behind,
not wanting to be left out of the race.
The girls jumped into the bed, climbing over the side,
Then into the cab they went to imagine a drive.

Suzy giggled, "Let's drive to the mall
and shop for some clothes!"
"Yes, let's go, I need new socks," laughed Melissa P.
Waterloaf.
After only ten minutes, Melissa P. Waterloaf thought t
hey should get food.
"Yes!" exclaimed Suzy. "Let's pretend to eat at the
Hungry Hamburger Dude."
Lou barked, Suzy clapped, and Melissa
P. Waterloaf put her hands in the air,
Oh, how the girls loved that truck that could
take them anywhere!
After more laughs and giggles, and pretending to eat,
The girls made one more pretend stop, to get a
pretend treat.
Off to the Malt Shop they went to get a milk shake,
The girls joked and said, "Mixing ten flavors
would be great."

Lou heard a dog bark, and jumped
across the front seat,
She stuck her nose out the window,
to bark loud and deep.
Melissa P. Waterloaf tried to grab her
and accidentally hit the gear shift,
The truck slipped into neutral and now
things were amiss.
When a car's put in neutral,
wheels can move without power,
This is why things got bad and quickly began to sour.
The truck rolled down the driveway,
first slow, then with speed,
Melissa P. Waterloaf said to Suzy,
"This is NOT what we need."
You should know the Waterloaf's house had a driveway,
steep and long,
And with an old truck backing down it,
things were bound to go wrong.

The girls turned around and saw the trouble
they were in,
As the truck picked up speed, their thoughts
were gone in the wind.
Lou was no help at all, all she did was bark and bark,
The girls began to get scared,
and hoped the truck would soon park.
In fact, things got much worse, as it began to sway.
Melissa P. Waterloaf and Suzy knew
it was time to be safe,
So they ducked down on the floor,
which was the safest place.

As the girls got down, Lou jumped a second time
across the seat,
And this time, SHE hit the gear shift.
What happened next was really neat!
The gear slipped into park and the truck
came to a quick stop,
If it had gone ten more feet,
there would have been a mess on the block.
Seconds after it stopped,
three cars came down the street,
The drivers would have had been angry
if they had been hit.
It took a few seconds before the girls
got up off the floor,
They hugged each other, kissed the dog,
then got out of the door.

Back into Melissa P. Waterloaf's house the girls went,
And decided to play, by building a huge, blanket tent.
Suzy stayed for dinner that night and the girls
shared their story,
Everyone decided Lou deserved all the glory.

The girls continued to play into the night,
With Lou by their side, everything was all right.

www.ingramcontent.com/pod-product-compliance
Lightning Source LLC
Chambersburg PA
CBHW041528120626
46551CB00018B/2613